THE Bear AND THE Star

BY
Lola M. Schaefer

ILLUSTRATED BY
Bethanne Andersen

Greenwillow Books
An Imprint of HarperCollinsPublishers

The Bear and the Star

Text copyright © 2019 by Lola M. Schaefer

Illustrations copyright © 2019 by Bethanne Andersen

All rights reserved. Manufactured in China.

For information address HarperCollins Children's Books,

a division of HarperCollins Publishers,

195 Broadway, New York, NY 10007.

www.harpercollinschildrens.com

Oil paints on gessoed Arches printmaking paper

were used to prepare the full-color art.

The text type is 26-point Weiss BT.

Library of Congress Cataloging-in-Publication Data

Names: Schaefer, Lola M., author. | Andersen, Bethanne, illustrator.

Title: The bear and the star / by Lola M. Schaefer ;

illustrated by Bethanne Andersen.

Description: First edition. | New York, NY : Greenwillow Books,

an imprint of HarperCollins Publishers, [2019] |

Summary: As a star rises higher and higher in the sky,

Bear finds the perfect tree, gathers animals to decorate it,

and summons people from around the world to join in a special celebration.

Identifiers: LCCN 2018006881 | ISBN 9780062660374 (hardcover)

Subjects: | CYAC: Holidays—Fiction. | Bears—Fiction. |

Animals—Fiction. | Peace—Fiction.

Classification: LCC PZ7.S33233 Be 2019 | DDC [E]—dc23

LC record available at https://lccn.loc.gov/2018006881

19 20 21 22 23 SCP 10 9 8 7 6 5 4 3 2 1

First Edition

Greenwillow Books

For those who share the light
—L. M. S.

To Theo Vincent Andersen,
who is a new peacemaker on the earth
—B. A.

$\mathcal{E}$arly one December morning,
Bear woke
and turned toward the horizon,
to a star—
a new star,
barely visible,
yet larger than any before.

It was time.

Bear stood and began his search
for a tree—
a tree that would be strong,

a tree that would be tall,
a tree that would be the center
of all to come.

And then, on the top of a windswept hill,
Bear found the tree—
an evergreen,
more majestic than any before.

Bear roared to the East,
then to the West.
He bellowed to the North,
then to the South.

And because it was time,
his call echoed
through canyon and valley,
between boulder and butte,
across prairie and lake.

Bear lumbered through the woods
and found squirrel and salamander,
cardinal and raccoon.

$\mathcal{A}$nd from everywhere,
animals came.

As the star shined brighter,
Bear *roared* louder than before,
his voice booming
across mesa and meadow,
over sea and peak,
from cliff and bluff.

People put down
hammer and hoe,
grass and thatch,
knife and rice,
shield and sword.

It was time.

Then they gathered
mask and drum,
scroll and shawl,
candle and copper,
flower and oil.

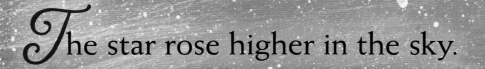

The star rose higher in the sky.

People brought friend
and neighbor,
son and daughter,
mother and father,
and faraway family

from city and farm,
across ocean and desert,
from mountain and island,

to the tree
that grew
stronger and taller
under a star—
a star larger and brighter than any before,
because it was time . . .

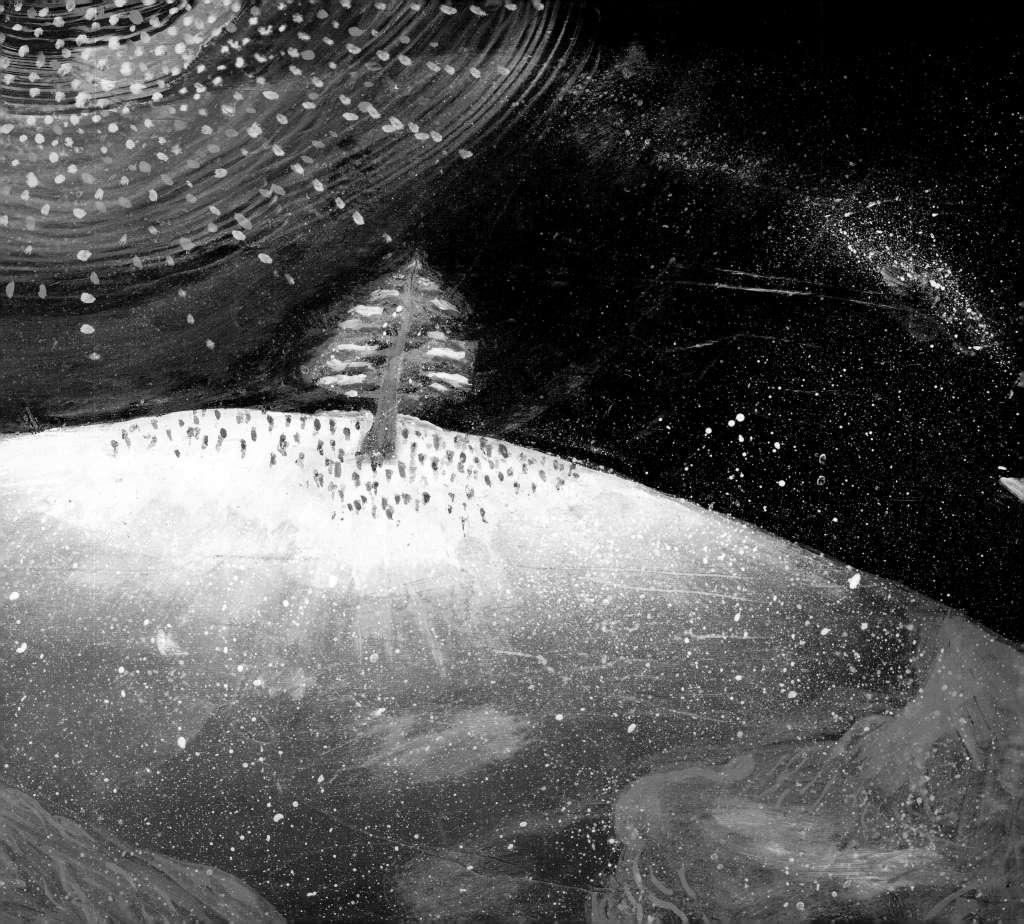

for
peace.